CUENTO DE LUZ

To my parents, my children, for Xabi . . . for you I wrote this story. I love you.
— Paula Merlán

To my parents, Nieves and Moisés; to my children, Elías and Sabela; and to Ramiro.
For all of you I would do anything.
— Blanca Millán

This book is printed on **Stone Paper©** that is Silver **Cradle to Cradle™** certified.

Cradle to Cradle™ is one of the most demanding ecological certification systems, awarded to products that have been conceived and designed in an ecologically intelligent way.

STONE PAPER®
NO TREES - NO WATER - NO BLEACH

Certified B Corporation®

Cuento de Luz™ became a **Certified B Corporation©** in 2015. The prestigious certification is awarded to companies which use the power of business to solve social and environmental problems and meet higher standards of social and environmental performance, transparency, and accountability.

For You
Text © 2021 Paula Merlán
Illustrations © 2021 Blanca Millán
© 2021 Cuento de Luz SL
Calle Claveles, 10 | Urb. Monteclaro | Pozuelo de Alarcón | 28223 | Madrid | Spain
www.cuentodeluz.com
Original title in Spanish: *Por vosotros*
English translation by Jon Brokenbrow
ISBN: 978-84-18302-09-1
1st printing
Printed in PRC by Shanghai Cheng Printing Company, January 2021, print number 1826-5

FOR YOU

PAULA MERLÁN   BLANCA MILLÁN

We would do anything for you . . .

We would eat all the vegetables, without grumbling.

We would sing a duet in the rain.

We would weave a boundless blanket of kisses with threads of joy.

We would bravely face up to all our fears.

We would magically solve all of your problems.

We would masterfully draw the path that leads to the stars . . .

Because you do anything for the two of us.

You keep us warm when it's cold outside.

Your smiles light up the way for us.

You are there to catch us when we fall.

Because you are always ready to lend a hand.

We would do anything to see you happy.

FOR YOU

Very happy!

Hugely
happy!

WORLD ART MAGAZINE

n° 192

Mom, Dad . . .

WE LOVE YOU
TO THE MOON
AND BACK!

ALL THE WAY TO
THE SUN
AND BEYOND
THE
STARS!